W9-CHP-623

ut Beginning Readers on the Right Track with ALL ABOARD READING™

he All Aboard Reading series is especially designed for beginning readers. Written by oted authors and illustrated in full color, these are books that children really *want* to ad—books to excite their imagination, expand their interests, make them laugh, and pport their feelings. With fiction and nonfiction stories that are high interest and rriculum-related, All Aboard Reading books offer something for every young reader. nd with four different reading levels, the All Aboard Reading series lets you choose hich books are most appropriate for your children and their growing abilities.

icture Readers

icture Readers have super-simple texts, with many nouns appearing as rebus pictures. the end of each book are 24 flash cards—on one side is a rebus picture; on the other de is the written-out word.

ation Stop 1

ation Stop 1 books are best for children who have just begun to read. Simple words d big type make these early reading experiences more comfortable. Picture clues lp children to figure out the words on the page. Lots of repetition throughout the xt helps children to predict the next word or phrase—an essential step in developing ord recognition.

ation Stop 2

ation Stop 2 books are written specifically for children who are reading with help. ort sentences make it easier for early readers to understand what they are reading. mple plots and simple dialogue help children with reading comprehension.

ation Stop 3

ation Stop 3 books are perfect for children who are reading alone. With longer text d harder words, these books appeal to children who have mastered basic reading skills. ore complex stories captivate children who are ready for more challenging books.

addition to All Aboard Reading books, look for All Aboard Math Readers™ (fiction ries that teach math concepts children are learning in school); All Aboard Science eaders™ (nonfiction books that explore the most fascinating science topics in e-appropriate language); All Aboard Poetry Readers™ (funny, rhyming poems for aders of all levels); and All Aboard Mystery Readers™ (puzzling tales where children ece together evidence with the characters).

l Aboard for happy reading!

For Grandma Sally and her crock of goofballs,
Otis, Jacob, Ella, Miles, and Lila—S.M.

For Nancy—B.B.

GROSSET & DUNLAP
Published by the Penguin Group
Penguin Group (USA) Inc., 375 Hudson Street, New York, New York 10014, U.S.A.
Penguin Group (Canada), 10 Alcorn Avenue, Toronto, Ontario, Canada M4V 3B2
(a division of Pearson Penguin Canada Inc.)
Penguin Books Ltd, 80 Strand, London WC2R 0RL, England
Penguin Ireland, 25 St Stephen's Green, Dublin 2, Ireland
(a division of Penguin Books Ltd)
Penguin Group (Australia), 250 Camberwell Road, Camberwell, Victoria 3124, Australia
(a division of Pearson Australia Group Pty Ltd)
Penguin Books India Pvt Ltd, 11 Community Centre, Panchsheel Park, New Delhi - 110 017, India
Penguin Group (NZ), Cnr Airborne and Rosedale Roads, Albany, Auckland 1310, New Zealand
(a division of Pearson New Zealand Ltd)
Penguin Books (South Africa) (Pty) Ltd, 24 Sturdee Avenue, Rosebank, Johannesburg 2196, South Africa

Penguin Books Ltd, Registered Offices:
80 Strand, London WC2R 0RL, England

Text copyright © 2005 by Stephen Mooser. Illustrations copyright © 2005 by Brian Biggs. All
rights reserved. Published by Grosset & Dunlap, a division of Penguin Young Readers Group,
345 Hudson Street, New York, New York 10014. ALL ABOARD MYSTERY READER and
GROSSET & DUNLAP are trademarks of Penguin Group (USA) Inc. Printed in the U.S.A.

Library of Congress Cataloging-in-Publication Data

Mooser, Stephen.
    Follow that flea! / by Stephen Mooser ; illustrated by Brian Biggs.
       p. cm. — (All aboard mystery reader. Station stop 3) (Goofball Malone ace detective)
    Summary: Second-grader Goofball Malone is known to be good with jokes, but he finally gets
his chance to be a detective when a dalmatian dog, Professor Pup, runs off from his owner.
    ISBN 0-448-43893-3 (pbk.) — ISBN 0-448-43894-1 (hardcover)
    [1. Dalmatian dog—Fiction. 2. Dogs—Fiction. 3. Jokes—Fiction. 4. Mystery and detective
stories.] I. Biggs, Brian, ill. II. Title. III. Series.
    PZ7.M78817Fo 2005
    [E]—dc22
                                            2004025127

(pbk)   10 9 8 7 6 5 4 3 2 1
(hc)   10 9 8 7 6 5 4 3 2 1

GOOFBALL MALONE
ace detective

FOLLOW THAT FLEA!

By Stephen Mooser
Illustrated by Brian Biggs

Grosset & Dunlap

Chapter 1: The Joker

My name is Chester Malone. But everyone calls me Goofball. Maybe it's because of my hair. It sticks out like porcupine quills. Or maybe it's my striped pants. Or it could even be my giant round glasses.

But probably it's because I tell jokes and riddles. Tons of them. More than anyone else in the second grade.

One afternoon, our class went to an
assembly in the auditorium. On the way
there, I got in line alongside my best
friend, Teensie Wigglesworth. She had a
bow on her head the size of a kite. She
thought it made her look tall. I thought
it made her look silly. But I never said so.
She was my best friend. She laughed at
everything I said.

"Guess what?" said Teensie. "I just learned to write with my left hand!"

"That's strange," I said. "I write with a pencil."

"You're silly," said Teensie.

"No, I'm Goofball," I told her. "You must be thinking of someone else."

Teensie laughed at my joke. She always did.

I wrote down the joke about the pencil in my red notebook. It said FUNNY THINGS on the cover. I used it all the time. It was filled with my favorite jokes and riddles. But the back pages of the book were still blank. Someday I was going to fill them up with lots of clues. I loved telling funny jokes, but more than anything, I wanted to be an ace detective. But so far, I had not found any mysteries to solve. So far.

Teensie and I walked into the auditorium. We sat down on a bench in the front row. The curtain was closed.

Whap! Someone clapped me on the back, hard. "Goofball! Move!"

It was Billy Puker. He was only one grade ahead of me but twice my size. He had a chipped front tooth. He had a pushed-in nose. He had a nasty attitude.

Teensie and I scooted over. Billy slid in. No one messed with Billy. Actually, only the teachers called him Billy. Everyone else called him Puke. He seemed to like the name.

Suddenly, the curtain opened. Everyone got quiet. A man wearing a tall hat stood in the middle of the stage. He had huge, bushy eyebrows. They looked just like furry caterpillars. To his right was a blackboard. To his left was a chair. Behind him were two doors. One door was marked number one. The other said number two.

The man tipped his hat. He bowed. "Good afternoon," he said. "My name is Doctor Fleaflicker. Who is the smartest one in the room?"

"I am!" exclaimed LuAnn Klack. She wanted to be Student of the Month.

"Teensie is!" I yelled. "She's a teensy bit smarter than LuAnn."

"Goofball is the smartest!" Teensie shouted.

Everyone laughed, including me.

"No, no, and no," said Dr. Fleaflicker. "The smartest one is Professor Pup!"

Just then door number one opened. Out ran a white puppy. He was covered with black spots. He jumped up onto the chair and sat down.

Dr. Fleaflicker went to the blackboard. He wiggled his eyebrows. The furry caterpillars did a little dance.

"Professor Pup here is the smartest dog in the world. He's worth a million dollars," said Dr. Fleaflicker.

Puke stood up. "A million bucks! Man, could I ever use a million bucks."

"Please sit down, Billy," one of the teachers said.

Puke sat down.

Up on the stage Professor Pup started
to scratch himself. So did Dr. Fleaflicker.
He scratched his neck. He scratched his
side. He even scratched under his arm.

"They both have fleas," I whispered to
Teensie. "Fleaflicker should flick some
off."

Teensie giggled.

"My dog can add," said Dr. Fleaflicker. "He can read. He can solve riddles. He can even speak English!"

"Prove it!" yelled Puke. "Show us."

"I will," said Dr. Fleaflicker. "But I want to warn you. You may not believe what you're going to see!"

Chapter 2: Dumb Riddles

Dr. Fleaflicker patted his dog. "Tell me, Professor, what is three plus three?"

The professor stopped scratching. Then he barked six times.

Everybody clapped. The professor wagged his tail.

"Here's a riddle," said the doctor. He stopped to scratch the back of his leg. "What is the best thing to put into a cake?"

The puppy pulled back his lips.

"That's right!" shouted Dr. Fleaflicker. "Your teeth are the best thing to put into a cake. Get it?"

I rolled my eyes. What a dumb riddle. I could do better. I pulled out my Funny Things book. I turned to page six. "Does he know this one?" I called out. "What do you call a skeleton that won't work?"

I didn't give Professor Pup a chance to answer.

"A lazybones!" I yelled.

Lots of people laughed. I stood up and waved. I was famous!

"Very good," said Dr. Fleaflicker. "Do you want to come up and write a riddle on the board?"

I didn't have to be asked twice. I was on the stage in a flash.

Dr. Fleaflicker whispered a riddle in my ear. I wrote it on the board. Who met Little Red Riding Hood in the woods?

Professor Pup tilted his head. He looked at the board, but he didn't speak. I don't think he knew the answer. Finally, Dr. Fleaflicker read the riddle out loud. "Who met Little Red Riding Hood in the woods?" At once, the professor answered, "Woof!"

"That's right—a wolf!" said Dr. Fleaflicker.

Everybody clapped. I bowed once more. Then I went back to my seat.

"Here's another great trick," said Dr. Fleaflicker. He wrote the number four on the board. "Professor Pup! Read that number."

The puppy tilted his head. Then he barked. Once.

"That's not right," said Dr. Fleaflicker
with a frown.

The dog barked again. Three times.

Dr. Fleaflicker started to get upset. He
waved four fingers in the professor's face.

"What is the answer?" he begged.

The dog didn't answer. A long time
went by.

"He's not so smart," Teensie whispered. "He doesn't know how to read."

"This show is like an angry skunk," I said.

"What do you mean, Goofball?" Teensie asked.

"I mean it's a real stinker!"

Teensie giggled.

Just then the bell rang. It rang loud. It rang long. School was out. But we didn't get up to leave. We were all waiting to see what Professor Pup would do next.

What he did next surprised everyone. With a yelp, he leaped up and jumped off the stage. Barking wildly, he raced down the aisle. Then he dashed out the front door.

"Catch him!" yelled Dr. Fleaflicker, waving his arms. "Don't let him get away. He's my best friend in the whole world. Somebody! Anybody! Help!"

Chapter 3: The Riddler

Dr. Fleaflicker jumped off the stage. "Professor, come back!" he yelled, running out the door.

Puke ran after him. We all followed after Puke. And why not? School was out for the day!

When I got outside, I spotted Dr. Fleaflicker standing on the steps. His face was bright red, and he was out of breath.

"My dog is gone!" he cried. "The bell must have scared him. I'll never see my little dog again." Dr. Fleaflicker looked ready to burst into tears.

Teensie looked like she might cry, too. "I'm sorry," she said.

"Poor me! I loved that little guy. He was the best dog ever," moaned Dr. Fleaflicker. He scratched at a flea behind his ear.

Teensie sniffled. I don't think she had ever heard such a sad story.

But what I heard was something else. Ever since I was five, I had wanted to be a detective. Up until now I never had a case to solve. But, suddenly, the case of the missing dog was licking me on the face.

Dr. Fleaflicker was chewing his nails and walking around in a circle.

"What are we going to do?" he moaned.

"Don't worry, Doc," I said. "I'll solve the mystery. I am Goofball Malone, Ace Detective."

"Goofball? That's a strange name for a detective," said Dr. Fleaflicker.

"I'm not joking," I said.

"I know you are not joking. You are Goofball," said Teensie. She giggled.

"No, listen," I said. "I am not just a joker. I am also a riddler."

"A riddler?" said Dr. Fleaflicker. He scratched his head. "How can a goofball riddler find my poor little puppy?"

"Riddles are little mysteries," I said. "And what just happened is a riddle. All we have to do is discover why that dog ran away. Then we can learn where he went."

"We can?" said Teensie.

"Really?" said Dr. Fleaflicker.

"I'm positive," I said. But deep down, my stomach was turning cartwheels. After all, it was my very first case.

Chapter 4: Not a Clue

Dr. Fleaflicker shook his head sadly. "What choice do I have? All right, Goofball! Find that dog!"

"Fat chance," said Puke as he walked by. "He's no detective. He's just a goofball."

Puke really knew how to hurt my feelings. I liked the name Goofball. But I did not like to be *called* a goofball. There's a big difference.

I glared at Puke. "Don't worry, Doc," I said. "That dog will be back in no time."

"I'm sure he will," said the doctor. But he didn't sound very sure.

I sat on the front steps of the school. Teensie sat down, too.

It was a beautiful day. The sky was blue. The air was sweet. The birds were singing.

But I was too busy to enjoy it. I had work to do.

I took out my Funny Things notebook. I turned to a blank page and wrote: Case of the Talking Dog. Then I wrote a riddle. Why did the talking dog run away?

"Because the bell scared him," said Teensie.

"Maybe," I said, writing it down.

"What else?" said Teensie.

I shrugged. I could not think of anything else.

I chewed on my pencil. I rubbed my chin. I sighed. This detective stuff was hard work.

"Poor Fleaflicker is in trouble and so is his dog," I said.

"Goofball, you're in trouble, too," said Teensie. "Everyone is counting on you."

Teensie was right. I had to find that dog. Otherwise I'd always be just Goofball. But if I found the dog, then I'd be Goofball Malone, Ace Detective. And that's who I wanted to be. More than anything.

Enough dreaming. Back to work. How could I solve this case? I didn't have a clue. Which, of course, was exactly what I needed.

I turned to another page in my book and wrote down: Clues. "Loud bell," I said. "Fleas," said Teensie. "Dog that talks but can't read," I said. "Tells silly riddles," said Teensie. "Black-and-white puppy," I said.

1. Loud Bell

2. Fleas

3. Dog that talks
   but can't read

4. Tells silly riddles

5. Black-and-white
   puppy

I put away my pencil and patted my book. "Now we are getting somewhere."

"We are?" said Teensie.

I stared at the clues. "Why did the dog run away?" I mumbled. "Why?" I stared at the clues some more. I tapped my head, hoping to shake loose an idea. But nothing popped up. I felt like someone had pointed a remote at my brain. Then pushed Mute.

Suddenly, my mouth fell open. The answer was right in front of my face! Clues one and five gave me the answer to the riddle!

Chapter 5: Hot on the Trail

"I know where the professor is!" I said, jumping up. "Clue one! Clue five!"

"Huh?" said Teensie.

I grabbed her hand and off we went down the street.

"Don't leave!" Dr. Fleaflicker shouted. "Where are you going?"

I stopped running and turned around. "Don't worry, Doc. The case is practically solved!"

I took off again. "Loud bell, black-and-white puppy," I said to Teensie. "Get it?"

"No," Teensie told me as we ran. Her big bow was flapping in the wind.

We flew down the street.

"Look out!" I yelled, scooting around a lady in a big hat.

"Scram!" said Teensie, waving at some pigeons sitting on the sidewalk. We passed LuAnn and her brother Buster. We passed

a teacher. We even passed Puke. He was
leaning against the window of Pee Wee's
Pet Shop. There was a big white bag at
his feet. We didn't say hello. We didn't say
good-bye. We ran and ran.

We ran past the laundry. It smelled
like soap. We ran past the flower stall. It
smelled like roses. We ran past the fruit
stand. It smelled like peaches. We ran so
hard that soon *I* smelled.

Luckily, we were done running. We had come to the fire station. A fire engine was parked in front. A firewoman was scratching her head. She made a face. I guess I still smelled.

"Teensie, think," I said. "What kind of dog is white with black spots?"

Teensie looked at the fire engine. Then she looked at the fire station. Then she looked at the firewoman.

"A firehouse dog?" she guessed.

"Right. A Dalmatian," I said.

"So?" said Teensie.

"So, Professor Pup is a Dalmatian! He probably made a mistake. He thought the school bell was a fire bell."

"I get it," said Teensie. "The fire dog wanted to go to the fire."

"That's right. He ran lickety-split to the closest fire station," I said.

I went up to the firewoman. She was busy itching.

"My name is Goofball Malone, Ace Detective," I told her. "I see you have fleas. I bet you got them from a little puppy."

The lady looked up. She kept on scratching. "I wish he had never come by. He jumped right onto the fire engine. I've been itching ever since."

"Hooray! The case is solved," I said. "Where is he?"

"When the dinner bell rang at the firehouse, he ran off," said the lady. "I haven't seen him since."

"Un-hooray!" I said. "Now the case is not solved."

"Do you know where he went?" asked Teensie.

"Probably home," she said. "For dinner."

"That dog should not be running around," I said. "He's worth a million dollars."

"Someone could steal him," Teensie added.

"Uh-oh," I said. "I just remembered something. Not really something—someone. Someone outside the pet shop."

I took out my notebook. I wrote down SUSPECTS. Only one name went onto the list: Puke.

Chapter 6: Follow That Flea!

We hurried back through town.

"Remember when Puke said he could use a million dollars?" I said.

"Sure. I could, too," said Teensie.

"Me too," I said. "But I wasn't standing in front of Pee Wee's Pet Shop just a little while ago holding a big bag. Maybe the professor was in the bag. Maybe Puke was going to sell him to Pee Wee."

Zoom, zoom. We passed the laundry, the flower stall, and the fruit stand. Teensie's bow was sagging to the side. But she didn't seem to notice.

Puke was leaning against the wall
between the laundry and the pet shop.
We skidded to a stop. The big white bag
was at his feet. But now it looked empty.
Maybe he had already sold the dog.

Puke looked up. He raised an eyebrow.
"What do you want, Goofball?"

I didn't answer right away. I wanted to
study my number-one suspect for clues.
If he had been near the professor, I was
about to find out.

"Beat it!" said Puke.

I stalled for time. I was waiting for him to make a move.

We stared into each other's eyes like cats on a fence. Neither one of us blinked.

A dryer was squeaking in the laundry. A parrot was squawking inside Pee Wee's.

Still, Puke didn't move.

"Beat it!" he repeated.

Finally, I spoke. "You passed the test. You didn't take him."

Teensie gasped. "But, Goofball." She paused to straighten her bow. "Aren't you going to ask him about Professor Pup?"

"He doesn't have him. Never did," I said. "Everybody who touched the professor got fleas. Puke didn't scratch once. He doesn't have the professor or his fleas."

Puke scowled. "You thought I had fleas?"

"What about that bag? It was filled with something when we came by before," said Teensie.

"Dirty clothes," I said. "I bet he's with his parents. They are probably doing laundry next door."

"You got a problem with that?" said Puke.

"No, but I do have a problem," I said. "Professor Pup is still missing."

Chapter 7: The Worst Detective

Teensie and I slowly headed back to school. I felt terrible. I was the world's worst detective. I probably could not have found my own ears.

Dr. Fleaflicker was sitting on the school steps. He looked up. His eyes were red from crying. "Tell me that you found him. Please," he begged.

"Sorry," I said. "The lady at the fire station said your puppy went home."

Dr. Fleaflicker groaned. "Home? That could be anywhere. We don't have a home."

"Why don't you have a home?" asked Teensie. Her bow was drooping like a thirsty flower. It looked ready to fall off her head.

"We don't have a home because of our job," said the doctor. "Every day we move to a new town. Every day we put on another show."

I took out my book. I wrote down *Clue #6: No home.*

The doctor sighed. "For the professor, home is not a house. Home is wherever his dish is."

"And where might that be?" I asked.

"In the dressing room, backstage," he said.

I quickly crossed out No home. Then I wrote in Backstage.

"Hooray!" I shouted. "The case is solved! The professor is in the dressing room!"

Chapter 8: The Ace Detective

We ran onto the stage. Someone had left the dressing room door open. The number one was on the door. I ran inside. Professor Pup's dish was on the floor. But Professor Pup was not there. This was no time to panic. I had to stay calm. I needed to be like curtains. I had to pull myself together.

I went over the clues once again. There was the answer—clue number three. It was practically poking me in the nose.

"Poor me," moaned Dr. Fleaflicker.

"Don't worry," said Teensie. She patted the doctor on the leg. "You can always get another dog."

Dr. Fleaflicker burst into tears. "But I don't want another dog!"

"And you won't have to get one," I said. "I'll say it again. The case is solved! The professor can't read. Remember? He can't tell the difference between one and two."

Teensie said, "So, Goofball, that means . . ."

"That means he's in room number two!" I shouted. "He went there by mistake."

"You could be on to something," said Dr. Fleaflicker. "I'm beginning to think you aren't really a goofball. You only look like one."

"Thanks," I said, "I guess."

The door to room number two was open. I ran inside. It was full of costumes. Piles of them. Pajamas here. Coats there. Hats and masks everywhere.

I swatted my arm. "He's here, all right. I just swatted a clue."

Chapter 9: The Talking Dog

The room was full of junk. Professor Pup could have been anywhere. Like inside a football helmet. Or behind a clown mask. Or even under a pile of ballerina tutus. It would take forever to dig through those clothes. I had to find him another way. Luckily, I knew what to do. I opened my book to page ten.

"Professor Pup," I said, "what grows on the outside of a tree?"

We heard a "bark" come from the back of the room.

"That's him!" said Teensie. Her bow was now hanging by a hair.

"Now answer this," I continued. "What is on top of a house?"

"Roof! Roof!" he replied. His voice was getting closer.

Finally, "How does sandpaper feel?"

"Ruff!" said the puppy. He bounded out from behind some rags.

The professor was back!

Dr. Fleaflicker bent over. He picked up his puppy. The professor licked the doctor's giant eyebrows. The doctor kissed him back. Then they both started scratching.

"Do everyone a favor," I said. "Please get that dog a flea collar."

"And the sooner the better," said Teensie. *Plop!* Her bow fell off her head.

I smiled. The professor was happy. The doctor was happy. And I was happy, too.

"Goofball, now you are an ace

detective," said Teensie. "Does that mean you will stop telling silly jokes?"

"Maybe," I said. "But, like a broken adding machine, don't count on it!"

Teensie laughed. What a good friend she was.

Dr. Fleaflicker slapped me on the back. "Goofball, you're the best detective in the world."

"And the funniest," said Teensie.

I smiled. I threw back my shoulders. I bet even my hair was standing straighter. "Mysteries are no laughing matter," I said. "But when I'm on the job, they will be."